1

CALLING
THE SHOTS

BY LOWERY CHRISTOPHER COLLINS

A COMEDY IN ONE ACT

CALLING THE SHOTS

A COMEDY IN ONE ACT

BY LOWERY CHRISTOPHER COLLINS

7

CALLING THE SHOTS,
A COMEDY IN ONE ACT

Written by Lowery Christopher Collins

Ponderlake Publishing: www.ponderlake.com

Playwright and/or Royalty Information: www.ChristopherCollinsOnline.com

ISBN 978-0-9992241-4-4

Ponderlake
Publishing

CALLING THE SHOTS

by Lowery Christopher Collins

CAST OF CHARACTERS (7M, 5F, 3 EITHER)

CHARLES BAGLEY—early 50's, mayor of a city

DANA BAGLEY—his wife, also early 50's

DURRY DURRANT—their domestic employee, a bit rough around the edges, world-weary, late 50's

APRIL BAGLEY—CHARLES and DANA's daughter, a free spirit, a bit wild, 20

REX WALTERS—APRIL's boyfriend, lives for REX, early 20's

WILLIAM BAINES—friend of REX and APRIL, early 20's

BETHANY HAYS—the Bagley's adolescent neighbor, suffers from multiple personalities

MARGOT SCHMITT—the mayor of Düsseldorf, Germany, 50's

WILHELM SCHMITT—her outgoing, narcoleptic son, early 20's

ALEX LEE MOORE—a film star, late 20's

LAUREN MANCHESTER—a film star, mid-20's

DETECTIVE OLAN CHAMBERLAIN—late 40's

OFFICER AJ HANKINS

OFFICER TERRY BLAYLOCK

A REPORTER

CALLING THE SHOTS

by Lowery Christopher Collins

Dana Bagley marches in from outside. She is dressed well and holds a purse. She is clearly angry.

She slams the door and paces.

A few moments later, her husband, Charles Bagley enters the room. He is quiet, but clearly not intimidated by her anger.

She stares at him and paces. He takes a seat and looks at her. After a while, she speaks.

DANA. Charles?

CHARLES. Yes.

DANA. Don't speak.

CHARLES. (*Clearly angered a little*) What?

DANA. I said, "Don't Speak." I don't want to hear it. (*Pause.*) What do you have to say for yourself?

CHARLES. Well, I . . .

DANA. I said, "Don't Speak."

CHARLES. Listen, I'm not . . .

DANA. I have never, never, never, never, never at any function, meeting, party, wedding, anything, anything at ALL been so embarrassed in my whole, entire, complete life. A funeral. A FUNERAL, CHARLES. A memorial service established to show honor, love, and respect to the dead. In a dignified way.

CHARLES. Okay.

DANA. Okay? Okay? You're unbelievable.

CHARLES. No, I'm a realist, and I'm honest.

DANA. That you are. Down to a fault.

CHARLES. That's what the people hired me to be. I didn't mince words with them, and I don't pretend.

DANA. But you're the mayor, Charles! The *mayor* of a world-class city! And you just stood in a three-acre cathedral during a funeral and laughed out loud.

CHARLES. It was funny.

DANA. It doesn't matter.

CHARLES. It was funny.

DANA. It was Victor Jordan's funeral, CHARLES, Victor Jordan, one of the most influential entrepreneurs and authors of our time.

CHARLES. I wasn't laughing at *him*.

DANA. (*Frustrating, walking away holding her forehead*) I *know*.

CHARLES. He was lying in the coffin, minding his own business.

DANA. I know.

CHARLES. I was laughing at his wife.

DANA. Oh, I *know*.

CHARLES. I've never seen someone just bust it right there in the aisle before.

DANA. I know.

CHARLES. And you know I held it in as long as I could.

DANA. Until you walked by the body.

CHARLES. And I did play it off as grief.

DANA. It didn't work. CHARLES, you broke into full laughter as you viewed the corpse of one of your biggest supporters.

CHARLES. People may not have noticed.

DANA. They may not have *noticed?!* Did you hear the collective gasp for air?

CHARLES. I passed it off as tears.

DANA. Charles.

CHARLES. She shouldn't have fallen.

DANA. She shouldn't have *fallen*?

CHARLES. It was distracting.

DANA. You think she tripped on purpose? At her husband's funeral?

CHARLES. I can't read others' thoughts.

DANA. You're impossible.

CHARLES. Look, I covered it up well. People thought I was crying.

DANA. If they were drunk.

CHARLES. Some were.

DANA. I give up.

CHARLES. The fact of the matter is it was a private funeral. No media. No recording devices. Just people and what they think they saw. We're safe. I promise.

DANA. The things I put up with.

CHARLES. You know it was funny.

DANA. Charles.

CHARLES. It was funny.

DANA. Charles!

CHARLES. Right?

DANA. Yes, it was. But that's not the point.

CHARLES. Exactly. It is exactly the point. I'm honest. It was funny. I tried. But, reality won. End of story.

DANA. You cannot bear to lose.

CHARLES. I don't lose. That's how I win.

DANA. Unbelievable.

CHARLES. And Mrs. Dana Bagley, that's why your husband is Charlie Bagley, the giant you see before you.

DANA. Well, giant of mine, just look out for boys named Jack carrying small axes. It's a long way to earth.

CHARLES. I intend to hold on to the goose, Dana.

Durry Durant enters.

DURRY. (*Hesitates at the door*) Is it safe to come in yet?

DANA. So, were you eavesdropping again, Durry?

DURRY. Not exactly, Mrs. Bagley. Just waiting to give you time to finish.

DANA. It comes from all sides and never ends.

CHARLES. Come on in, DURRY.

DURRY. Good. I got tired of standing out there. (*He sits.*) The ol' legs ain't what they used to be. You know, back in the army, they used to make us march for hours on end, but I was just nineteen, so I could do just about anything. A few years later . . .

DANA. Durry, don't you have work to do?

CHARLES. Dana, that's just rude.

DANA. He's our employee!!!

DURRY. That's okay, Mr. Bagley. She's right. I'm on the clock. (*Stands.*) I parked the car in the garage. I could probably find a few things that need finishing here and there.

April, Rex, and William enter. April and Rex are all over each other. Everyone else in the living room watches—in a bit of disgusted shock.

DANA. Hello, darling.

APRIL. Oh, hello, Mom, Dad, Durry.

CHARLES. Nice to have you home. Still living in the dorm across town that I'm paying for?

APRIL. Of course, I am, but I have to stop in here to see my amazingly generous, successful parents.

CHARLES. What do you want?

APRIL. Nothing. Seriously. Just stopping in to see if you have anything to eat.

CHARLES. Ah.

DANA. And how are you, Rex?

CHARLES. Covered with love.

REX. I'm good, Mrs. Bagley. How are you today?

DANA. Having a wonderful day, just a Nutter-Butter day. Wouldn't you agree, Charles?

CHARLES. I don't agree easily. Rex, had enough of my daughter yet? I'd figure a year was enough.

APRIL. Daddy! Ignore him, Rex.

REX. One year down, seventy to go.

CHARLES. Oh, for a short life.

APRIL. We are delightfully happy.

DANA. Delightfully.

CHARLES. Happy.

DURRY. Wow.

CHARLES. You'll learn.

CHARLES. And, William, is it?

WILLIAM. Yes, sir.

CHARLES. How are you?

WILLIAM. I'm fine, sir.

CHARLES. Good to hear. And you can dispense with the "sirs." I appreciate it, but you don't have to do that.

WILLIAM. Yes, sir. Oh, sorry. Okay.

DURRY. I'm going in the kitchen to start some coffee. Do you want something to eat, April?

APRIL. Absolutely, Durry. I'm starving to death.

CHARLES. I'm glad we have a large pantry.

DANA. And it's full. Come on, April. Charles, guys, let's see what we can find to eat. Maybe it'll clear my thoughts.

CHARLES. All it takes is a gentle clap of thunder.

DANA. Charles!

CHARLES. I'm the mayor.

DANA. I'm the queen. Come eat.

Everyone, except Rex and William, start to exit toward the kitchen.

CHARLES. Come on, boys. Want some food?

REX. We'll be there in a minute, Mr. Bagley.

CHARLES. Suit yourself.

Only Rex and William remain.

REX. Did you hide it?

WILLIAM. I did my best.

REX. What does that mean? If anyone finds it, we're dead. But this would be the last place anyone would look for it. I tried to keep April occupied for you.

WILLIAM. You did that.

REX. What?

WILLIAM. Nothing. I put it under a brick in the edging of the shrubs along the right side of the drive.

REX. Hidden?

WILLIAM. Yeah. Nobody can see it. It's under a brick.

REX. Good. We don't need to have anyone see us with a handgun of any kind.

WILLIAM. I still don't feel right about hiding it here.

REX. Just for a little while. And think about it. It's the mayor's house, William.

WILLIAM. April would die.

REX. April need not know. I satisfy her enough to keep her curiosity down. Oh, how many did we get last night?

WILLIAM. What?

REX. Focus, my boy. How many did we get last night?

WILLIAM. People or locations?

REX. People.

WILLIAM. Three, seven, ten, fourteen. Fourteen.

REX. Fourteen. All of them right between the eyes.

WILLIAM. Rex, this is fun and all, but I think we need to be careful. Some people wouldn't understand. They might think we're violent or something.

REX. We're pretty good shots.

WILLIAM. Yeah, we are. It's more fun than I've ever had. I just don't want to get caught.

REX. Just relax. I'm calling the shots. Anyway, it's just all good fun. Nobody's getting hurt. We shoot a few movie stars right between the eyes. It's not like it kills 'em. They're just posters. The theaters can afford new ones. They're rich. It's just fun. Just fun.

WILLIAM. I guess so.

REX. You know so. (*Pause.*) Let's go eat.

WILLIAM. Go on. I'll be there in a minute.

WILLIAM. (*Picks up a photograph off of a table*) Oh, April. What do you see in him? Everybody hates him, even me. You can do so much better.

DURRY enters.

DURRY. What are you doing, mate?

WILLIAM. (*Startled*) Nothing. Just looking at everything.

DURRY. We have grub in the galley, boy.

WILLIAM. I know. Thank you.

DURRY. No need to be fretful over something you can't fix, right?

WILLIAM. I'm going to eat now.

DURRY. You do that. You do that. (*William exits.*)

DANA enters with flamboyance.

DANA. When did they say it happened, Charles?

CHARLES follows.

CHARLES. What, my little urchin?

DANA. When did they say the shootings happened?

CHARLES. Early this morning.

DURRY. Shootings?

DANA. Yes!

DURRY. Somebody hurt?

CHARLES. No, somebody's shooting out the faces on the movie posters again.

DURRY. Again?

DANA. Yes! That makes the third time! I think it's pathetic and it's an omen. There's something behind it. I just know it.

CHARLES. It seems there is a pattern.

DANA. And it's blight upon your city, Charles, an absolute blight!

CHARLES. I know, Dana.

DANA. I worry about public perception.

CHARLES. Okay, Dana! I know.

DANA. You hate me.

CHARLES. Yes, I do. If I didn't hate you, I would never have married you.

DANA. What about the center?

CHARLES. I know.

DANA. It's your legacy.

CHARLES. I know.

DANA. For years, you have wanted to build the Charles Bagley Center for the Performing Arts.

CHARLES. Are you narrating?

DANA. With style and clarity. Theatre, art, concerts, film festivals, everything you've wanted in jeopardy because of vandals shooting movie posters at 3 a.m.

Charles stares at Dana.

DANA. What?

CHARLES. Are you finished?

DANA. What?

CHARLES. *(to Durry)* Is she finished?

DURRY. Probably not.

CHARLES. Why couldn't they just shoot Rex? He's a waste of space.

DANA. As much as I agree, this isn't the time.

CHARLES. It's always the time for truth. Rex rhymes with "sex," and that makes me uncomfortable.

DANA. Charles, April is a grown woman . . .

CHARLES. Stop. Stop. Some truth is never to be spoken.

DURRY. I remember when I was about twenty or twenty-one. Me and my friends hopped a freighter to Amsterdam. It took a year to get rid of that . . .

CHARLES. Durry. Durry, never, never mention any of your childhood diseases.

DANA. I think I just threw up a little.

The doorbell rings. Everyone just stands.

DANA. Durry? (*open hand to the door*)

DURRY goes to the door. Standing there is BETHANY, the fifteen-year-old next-door neighbor.

Durry looks back at the couple with a look of disgust.

BETHANY. (*With a deep raspy voice*) Hello, darlings.

DANA. Heaven help.

DURRY. What are you doing here, Bethany?

BETHANY. Bethany? Who is this Bethany? I don't know a Bethany. I suppose Bethany may be a fifteen-year-old next-door neighbor to the illustrious mayor, but I am not she.

DANA. My stomach hurts.

CHARLES. If you'd go on a diet, you'd be okay.

BETHANY. Charles, Charles, Charles. You know you are just being cruel. Act your age, man.

CHARLES. Go home.

DURRY. Bethany . . .

BETHANY. I am Samantha, owner of the phenomenal Club 87 on 78th Street.

CHARLES. Go home. Durry?

DURRY. (*Shoving her out of the door*) Go home, BETHANY Samantha.

DANA. Did we buy a home on crazy row?

Charles shakes his head and exits toward the kitchen. Dana places her fingers on her forehead—as if she nursing a headache—and follows shortly behind Charles. Durry looks around, shrugs his shoulders and heads toward the terrace. As soon as the room is clear, April and Rex enter hand-in-hand, "plop" onto the couch and start making out. Charles enters as if he forgot something in the living room, sees the pair, and shows disgust.

CHARLES. For the love of Pete, do you have to do that?

APRIL. Oh, Daddy. I'm a grown woman. I enjoy the company of men.

CHARLES. Why are you with Lord Farquaad then?

APRIL. Daddy!

CHARLES. April, I have come to some painful realities about you, realities I have subsequently blocked out of my mind as untruths. Don't shatter my lies with evidence of truth. Please. It's all a father asks.

REX. Mr. Bagley.

CHARLES. Don't speak. Good Lord, I sound like Dana.

REX. Mr. Bagley . . .

CHARLES. No. Just don't do that here. And Rex, sex, or whatever your name is, when you decide to die, give me a two-minute warning. I have some popcorn for the microwave.

APRIL. Daddy!

CHARLES. I am going to call the Chief to see if they know any more about the posters.

He starts to exit, and WILLIAM enters.

WILLIAM. Mr. Bagley, how are you?

CHARLES. Wishing there were a Santa Claus, WILLIAM, wishing there were a Santa Claus.

He exits.

WILLIAM. What was that all about?

REX. Ah, he caught us going at it?

WILLIAM. What?

APRIL. Rex!

REX. Not going at *it*, just making out.

WILLIAM. Oh.

REX. Cheer up, my boy. You worry too much. It's no big deal. Right, April?

APRIL. It'll pass.

WILLIAM. What did he mention about posters?

REX. Nothing.

APRIL. Evidently, someone's been shooting out the faces of the movie posters again.
(*WILLIAM looks guiltily at REX, who tries to get him to stop doing so.*) I hope they
can find who's doing it. To begin with, it was kind of funny, but now it's getting the
wrong kind of attention. It could hurt Daddy's chances of getting his performing arts
center built.

WILLIAM.   What?

REX. She doesn't mean it.

APRIL. What do you mean? Of course, I mean it. He's worked on this for years. It's part of
his goals as mayor, that and strengthening his bonds with our German sister city,
Düsseldorf.

REX. Is this a narrative?

APRIL. Yes. But it all may be lost now.

WILLIAM. That's horrible.

REX. It's okay.

APRIL. No, it's not.

REX. How do you know things are as bad as that?

APRIL. I eavesdrop well. I have heard the conversations, the phone calls.

WILLIAM. This isn't good.

REX. April, let's go for a drive.

APRIL. A drive?

REX. I need some fresh air, and I need to ride around.

WILLIAM. Do I . . . ?

REX. We'll be back. We're not leaving you. (*He walks over to WILLIAM, hand on shoulder.*) It'll be okay, William, my boy. It's all good.

APRIL. I need to stop by the drug store. There are a few things I need to pick up.

REX. I'm sure.

WILLIAM. I'll be here.

REX. Later, bro.

APRIL. See you in a bit, William. Hold down the fort.

Rex and April leave.

WILLIAM. Good bye, April. Oh, that you would see me for me.

DURRY walks in.

DURRY. Yep. Just as I figured.

WILLIAM. (*Startled*) What?

DURRY. You know.

WILLIAM. I don't know anything.

DURRY. That's probably true, but it's not the point.

WILLIAM. I need to go.

DURRY. Look. I'm on your side, boy. I like you. You're a slight bit better than that moron she's with now.

WILLIAM. I . . . (*Stammers*)

DURRY. Calm down. It's all right. You love her, don't you?

WILLIAM. I don't . . . I can't . . .

DURRY. If it's true, just say yes. It's okay. You're a good man.

WILLIAM. (*Hesitates.*) Yes.

DURRY. Exactly. Truth. Finally. Look, the Bagleys don't like the little snot either. Let me see what I can do about it.

WILLIAM. What?

DURRY. Do you love her?

WILLIAM. Yes.

DURRY. Let me do what I do.

WILLIAM. I don't know.

DURRY. There ain't nothing to know. Go get you something to eat. Let DURRY take care of things. That's what I do. I'm pretty good at calling the shots.

WILLIAM. I'm . . .

DURRY. You're hungry. Go get you some food. Go.

WILLIAM walks away in a daze.

DURRY. Now to decide which way to go. It's been a long time since I took care of someone, especially for the sake of true love.

DANA walks in from the terrace.

DANA. What are you doing?

DURRY. Plotting a death.

DANA. You, too? (*Pause*) Where is everyone?

DURRY. April and the ass are out. That William boy is in the kitchen. Mr. Bagley's in his office, on the phone with the governor.

DANA. Good. (*looking around guiltily*) Have you heard from Chicago?

DURRY. Yep.

DANA. And?

DURRY. Everything is good to go.

DANA. They paid the full amount?

DURRY. They bet the full amount.

DANA. Bingo.

DURRY. Don't count your chickens . . .

DANA. It always turns out. No matter what, we get our share.

DURRY. That's why we're bookies.

DANA. Shhh.

DURRY. What?

DANA. This still can't get out.

DURRY. What? That the former bookie and current wife of one of the most influential mayors in the country is running a multi-million-dollar gambling ring right out of the mayoral home?

DANA. What is this? Narrative?

DURRY. Something like that.

DANA. I just don't want this out.

DURRY. You enjoy the money?

DANA. (*Hesitates.*) Yes.

DURRY. You got in here, pretending to hate me all the way. It's a perfect cover. We've got a good thing going: a friendship based in money.

DANA. I know. We just have to be careful. (*Pause*) Chicago did call?

DURRY. Yep.

DANA. The full amount?

DURRY. Yep.

DANA. Okay.

The doorbell rings again. DURRY goes to answer it. BETHANY is there again.

BETHANY. Umm. Hello.

DURRY. What do you want, loon girl?

BETHANY. Uh… could you help me find my mommy?

DANA. Bethany, do I need to call your mother?

BETHANY. You know my mommy? My name is Sally, and I am lost.

DANA. Bethany, just walk home.

DURRY. I'm not a patient man.

DANA. Durry, let's try to . . .

DURRY. No. Go home. (*He slams the door. It doesn't close fully.*)

During the course of the next conversation, it is obvious that APRIL has returned and eavesdrops.

DANA. You know how embarrassing it is to live next door to a girl like that?

DURRY. Uh, yes.

DANA. I used to think she was faking, just trying to get attention, but I've grown to believe that she's out of her mind.

DURRY. Aren't we all?

DANA. Oh, Durry. Do you know how difficult it is to pretend that I don't like you? All the lies, making Charles think that I hate the fact that he hired you when I was responsible for manipulating him into it all along.

DURRY. We have a good thing going, Chica. Let's not screw it up. I don't want to go back to the way things were, the lonely rooms, the loose women. Well, I miss some of it, but that's beside the point.

DANA. Stop while you're ahead, Durry. If I didn't love you so much, I'd slap you. Remember, all this stays with us. Charles can never know.

DURRY. Well, duh.

DANA. Let's go find Charles, separately of course.

DURRY. Whatever.

They exit.

April walks in stunned.

APRIL. (*to herself*) Mommy? Mommy and Durry?? Ewww. Mommy? Durry? That's where I get it?

William enters.

WILLIAM. Hey, April. Where's Rex?

APRIL. (*Distracted*) Who?

WILLIAM. Rex?

APRIL. Oh, he dropped me off. He had to run back to the drug store. He paid for his anti-diarrheal medication, but he forgot it there.

WILLIAM. His *what*?

APRIL. What?

WILLIAM. Uh.

APRIL. William, what am I going to do??

WILLIAM. What? What's wrong?

APRIL. I just . . .

WILLIAM. What?

APRIL. I just overheard . . .

WILLIAM. What?

APRIL. I just overheard my mom and Durry talking . . .

WILLIAM. What?

APRIL. I think they're having an affair.

WILLIAM. Your mom and Durry?

APRIL. I heard it with my own ears.

WILLIAM. Wow. I'm sorry.

APRIL. I don't know what to say.

WILLIAM. There is really nothing to say.

APRIL. Oh, William. (*She cries on his shoulder. He is shocked.*)

WILLIAM. Oh . . . April?

APRIL. I always thought I could handle anything, but I'm in shock.

WILLIAM. Me, too?

APRIL. Oh, William, you are so sweet, so understanding. Rex would just have some smart remark and to try to be funny.

WILLIAM. Uh huh.

APRIL. I mean . . .sometimes I don't think he understands me at all. He's just interested in one thing.

WILLIAM. Okay.

APRIL. It gets old. A man like you wouldn't be that way.

WILLIAM. No?

APRIL. Not all guys are alike. I'm not blind.

WILLIAM. No?

APRIL. Not at all. Some guys are different. Some guys are just good.

WILLIAM. Yeah?

APRIL. Yeah. And I know you're one of them. William, you're a sweetheart.

WILLIAM. I?

APRIL. Of course, you.

WILLIAM. Uh . . .

APRIL. It's okay, William. (*She kisses him on the cheek.*) I have some changes to make. Big changes.

April walks out. William stands in shock.

WILLIAM.   Is Durry a magician?

The doorbell rings. MARGOT Schmitt, mayor of Düsseldorf, Germany and her narcoleptic son, WILHELM, is standing in the doorway.

MARGOT.   Hello!

WILLIAM.   Hello?

MARGOT.   Hello, and you are the what you say butler?

WILLIAM.   What?

MARGOT.   The butler?

WILHELM.   The one who answers the door for the house.

WILLIAM.   Oh, no. I'm a friend of the family.

MARGOT.   Ah, hello, friend of the family. My name is Margot Schmitt. I am mayor of your European sister city, Düsseldorf, Germany. And this is my son by the name of Wilhelm, Wilhelm Schmitt, he shares my final name.

WILLIAM.   Your final . . . ?

WILHELM.   Hello, friend. Sometimes you want to go where everybody knows your name, eh? Cheers, friend. Hello.

WILLIAM.   Uh, yeah. Would you like to come in?

MARGOT.   It's time you ask. May I ask what you call yourself, friend of Charles Bagley?

WILLIAM.   William.

MARGOT.   William? Wonderful! That is the name also of my son here, Wilhelm.

WILLIAM.   Ah, good.

WILHELM.   Hello, William, American who shares my name.

WILLIAM.   Are you here to see Mr. Bagley? I can see if I can find him.

MARGOT.   Yes, we are here to make ourselves an official visit. CHARLES will be not be expecting us. He does not know that we have come to America, but we are here for

31

several reasons, so I wanted to make a stop in our sister city and see my counterpart. Our driver is waiting in the car.

WILLIAM. Let me go and . . .

Wilhelm falls out.

WILLIAM. What's wrong?

MARGOT. (*Looking after her son calmly*) It's okay, William. He will be fine. He goes out from time to time. He has what you call dyssomnia or narcolepsy. He just sleeps.

Durry enters.

DURRY. What's going on here?

WILLIAM. Durry, this is just . . .

DURRY. Did you kill someone?

WILLIAM. No, I . . .

DURRY. Frau Schmitt. What a surprise.

MARGOT. Ah, Durry. What a pleasant surprise to see you.

DURRY. Is something wrong?

MARGOT.   Wilhelm is just dropping off again.

WILLIAM. What is this? Six degrees of separation?

MARGOT. Six degrees?

DURRY. I've known Mr. Bagley a long time.

CHARLES.   (*Entering*) A very long time. What's . . . ?

MARGOT. Charles!

CHARLES.   Margot. I had no idea.

MARGOT.   Neither did we.

WILHELM. *Mutter?*

MARGOT. *Dies ist deine Mutter.*

WILHELM. *Ich möchte Wasser.*

MARGOT. Durry, can I trouble you a bit for some water?

WILLIAM. I'll get it. (*Leaves*)

WILHELM. (*Standing up*) Sorry for the scare that I gave your way. I have a bit of a problem that jumps upon me.

MARGOT. *Sind sie ok?*

WILHELM. *Ja.*

CHARLES. So, in the midst of everything else, to what do I owe the honor of this pleasure?

MARGOT. Well, I had to come to America for some meetings in New York and in Baltimore. I hate to come here without visiting our sister city. And Henry heard I was in town so he arranged some meetings downtown at the Plaza. And I have to see my Charles Bagley.

DANA. (*Entering*) Margot Schmitt.

MARGOT. The other Bagley.

DANA. (*Sophisticated hug*) Margot. What a surprise. I had no idea.

MARGOT. I was just telling Charles that we had an unexpected trip here. And I brought Wilhelm!

DANA. Oh, Wilhelm. Need a cot?

WILHELM. (*Smiling*) DANA Bagley.

MARGOT. Love the American humor.

CHARLES. We're here all week.

MARGOT. CHARLES, can I ask of you a special favor? Those papers we had drawn up when you and DANA came over, when I met you in Hannover? Do you still have those? And the drawings?

CHARLES. Yes, why?

MARGOT. May I see them please? I just want to check on something.

CHARLES. It requires walking.

DANA. Charles.

CHARLES. Only joking. Care to join me, Margot?

MARGOT. No, I'll stay here and have chat with the better half of the Bagleys.

CHARLES. The better half?

MARGOT. You don't fool me, Charles. I know you love this woman.

CHARLES. I only married her because I thought she was pregnant. Turns out it was only indigestion. I've lived with the heartburn for twenty-five years.

WILHELM. Oh, I get that one. That statement is on the fence of humorous. I like this humor very much.

CHARLES. Glad to be your Leno.

WILHELM. I get that one, too! You get funnier each trip, Mr. Bagley.

CHARLES. I'll be back.

WILHELM. And that one!!

CHARLES. That wasn't one. Calm down. (*Starts to leave*) On second thought, don't calm down too much. The furniture has sharp edges. (*Leaves*)

The front door bursts open. BETHANY appears! She carries a tennis racket.

BETHANY. Oh, dear. How is everyone today?

DANA. Dear Lord.

BETHANY. Oh, Elizabeth, Franklin, however are you? I am just getting ready for my first set. (*She hugs MARGOT.*)

MARGOT. Do I know . . .

DANA. No. she. . .

DURRY. Go!

WILHELM. What's wrong.

DURRY. Go home, Bethany, or I will call your mom to bring a net.

DANA. Durry!

MARGOT. I am confused. Is there something wrong with this girl?

BETHANY. With what girl? Is there a girl here?

DANA. Margot, I am so sorry. Bethany here . . .

BETHANY. Why do I keep hearing the name Bethany everywhere I go? This is getting quite odd?

DURRY. I'm going to get my bat.

DANA. Durry, no need for displays of sport.

BETHANY. Is no one coming to watch me play? If I advance today, I travel to Wimbledon.

WILHELM. Oh, she is what you call bonkers then?

BETHANY. What?

MARGOT. Ah!

WILHELM. Next-door neighbor? I am so sorry. Rich and crazy.

DURRY. Yeah. the ticket to your own reality show on TV.

DANA. Bethany, I need you to go home now.

BETHANY. Bethany? My name is . . .

DANA. Exactly.

BETHANY. But I need to play my match.

DANA. There are plenty matches at home. Go strike them up. Good bye.

Dana gently manages to get Bethany out of the door.

WILHELM. What a significant twist.

DURRY. You ain't seen nothing.

MARGOT. Before Charles returns, I have to ask you both something.

DANA. Certainly.

MARGOT. Has either of you heard from Chicago?

DANA. (*Looking around*) Shhh. Chicago?

MARGOT. Yes, don't forget, Dana. I am taking care of everything on the other side of the
        pond.

DANA. I know. It's just there are so many people here today.

MARGOT. I know, and I am sorry. I just wanted to check before I call Warsaw and Vienna.
        There's a lot at stake. No one is going to get hurt in any of this. It's a win-win from
        our standpoint.

DANA. (*Happy*) I think so, too, Margot. There's a lot to be made. And I do hope to be able
        to help Charles without his even knowing it.

MARGOT. So?

DURRY. Yeah. Chicago's a go.

MARGOT. Excellent.

WILHELM. Wonderful!

DANA. We just need to change the subject soon.

MARGOT. I know. I do need to look at those plans. I think we can coordinate with you guys to
        get what I need in Düsseldorf as well. You never know, we may even get the
        Olympics one day. We get Winter and you get Summer. It's a good deal with a lot
        of money to be made.

DANA. I hope so. I think it's really possible. Sometimes you have to learn to use the system in
        way many people would never understand. That's why I have learned to trust Durry so
        much. He knows how. (*She puts her hand on Durry's shoulder. April walks in and
        pauses.*)

APRIL. Oh.

DANA. What? (*Removes hand*)

APRIL. Nothing.

DANA. What?

APRIL. Nothing, mother. Nothing.

DURRY. Mrs. Bagley, I do know how to fix that garbage disposal. I'm sorry it didn't work for you. I'll go fix it. (*He exits.*)

APRIL. And who are these dignitaries we share our lives with?

DANA. April, you remember Margot Schmitt, mayor of Düsseldorf, and her son, Wilhelm?

APRIL. Oh, of course, I am so sorry. You hosted us at your home.

MARGOT. Yes, we did.

APRIL. I'm so sorry. I have a lot on my mind right now. Decisions, lies, betrayals, disillusionments, sorrow.

DANA. What's wrong, April.

APRIL. Nothing. You go back to entertaining. (*She sits.*)

DANA. I'm sorry, Margot. She's been acting a bit strange recently.

WILHELM. Oh, I understand. It's the pressures of being the second generation of the people who shape the things we see. It's normal for us to be strange.

He sits beside April.

APRIL. Hello?

WILHELM. Hello, April. I remember when you were in Düsseldorf. We talked by the pool.

APRIL. I remember.

WILHELM. I knew you would.

APRIL. All of your friends were swimming naked. How could I not remember?

WILHELM. What do you mean?

WILLIAM enters.

APRIL. Naked. Everyone was naked. You were naked.

WILHELM. We were swimming. (*Sits closer*) We do things different in Europe.

APRIL. You were naked. It's hard to forget a conversation like that.

WILHELM. Unforgettable, huh? So, you remember me naked? Still think about it?

WILLIAM. Hello, April.

APRIL. (*Stands*) Oh, hi, William.

WILLIAM. What's going on?

WILHELM. Just talking about me naked.

APRIL. (*Puts her arm around William.*) It's nothing. Wilhelm, have you met William yet.
William is my . . .

Rex enters.

REX. Your what?

APRIL. My dear friend. (*Walks to Rex*) Oh, Rex. (*Kisses him on the cheek*) William was just
helping me, I mean, talking to Wilhelm with me.

REX. Wilhelm?

APRIL. Yes. This is Wilhelm.

DANA. The son of the mayor of Düsseldorf, Germany, Frau Schmitt.

MARGOT. Which would be me.

REX. I go to pick up some medicine and come back and wow.

WILLIAM. Some anti-diarrheal medication?

REX.   Some what? (*Looks at April*) No! Some . . . aspirin.

DANA. Oh, I had some aspirin.

MARGOT. So did I. (*Digs in her purse*)

REX. No, it's okay. I got what I needed from the drug store.

CHARLES. (*Entering*) Why do I walk in at these times?

REX. Hello, Mr. Bagley.

CHARLES. I found the papers, Margot. What do you need to see?

MARGOT. I was thinking Olympics, Charles.

WILHELM. (*to William*) I am capable of many sports.

WILLIAM. I don't care.

WILHELM. (*Standing up*) Baseball. (*He pretends to play baseball.*) What you call soccer. (*Acts it out*) Basketball. (*Acts it out*) Swimming. (*Takes off shirt, pretends*)

CHARLES. There's really no need.

WILHELM. The warm water. (*He passes out on April. She is forced to catch him. William goes to her aid, letting Wilhelm drop.*)

MARGOT. Oh, don't let him fall. (*Running to his aid*)

APRIL. What was that?

WILLIAM. Narcolepsy.

REX. *Narco* what?

WILLIAM. Narcolepsy.

The doorbell rings. DANA answers.

Lauren Manchester and Alex Lee Moore are at the door. They apparently are well-known young actors.

DANA. Hello. Oh.

APRIL. Lauren Manchester? Alex Lee Moore?

They smile, weakly.

REX. What?

APRIL. You're Lauren and Alex Lee?

ALEX LEE. The last time we checked.

MARGOT. Who's what?

APRIL. Just two of the biggest movie stars alive today. And they are here on my doorstep.

WILHELM. Did someone say "movie star," eh?

LAUREN. I hope we didn't come at a bad time.

ALEX LEE. Don't be ridiculous. There isn't any such thing.

APRIL. Oh, my. Come in.

DANA. Yes, come in.

ALEX LEE. Is Bagley here?

CHARLES. Which Bagley are you wanting?

ALEX LEE. Oh, okay. Charles, there you are.

CHARLES. The last time I checked.

ALEX LEE. We need to talk.

CHARLES. About what?

ALEX LEE. Lauren and I . . .

APRIL. Stars of the current hit, *My Widow and Me*!

ALEX LEE. Yeah. Anyway, Lauren and I have both been pushing for this center. I mean movies are the money makers, but we both love serious acting. You know Redford had his Sundance, but together, a handful of us could turn the Bagley into a big, big, big venture, making not only money, but stars, concreting certain names into stone forever. You know what I'm saying, Bagley.

CHARLES. I guess *you're* a narrator, too.

ALEX LEE. And you know what happened last night in your own city, Charles?

CHARLES. I can only guess.

ALEX LEE. *We* got shot: Lauren and I, our faces out of three posters. I can handle good clean fun, but that scares me, Charles.

APRIL. Those shooters ought to be killed.

REX. That's going a little far, don't you think, baby?

APRIL. Not at all. I am tired of deception of all types. Why can't people just be honest?

WILLIAM. I agree.

REX. Shut up.

DANA. No need to be rude.

ALEX LEE. I'm a supporter, Charles. I think this has amazing potential, but this doesn't look right—and then those people out by your street holding up those signs.

CHARLES. What signs? (*looking out*)

ALEX LEE. Something about laughing, "showing some respect" or something.

DANA. Are you serious? (*looking*) Charles.

The doorbell rings. Everyone is startled.

Dana answers it. It's a reporter.

REPORTER. Hello, I'm Kelly Harken from the Evening Post. I wanted to ask Mr. Bagley a few questions if possible.

DANA. Uh, this is his home. Could you please go to his office?

REPORTER. Well, I did go there, and they told me that he was here and conducted a lot of city business from these premises. Then the protesters were out of the curb, and I thought I would at least come and ask Mr. Bagley directly before I wrote the story for tomorrow's edition, trying to be fair.

DANA. Well . . .

CHARLES. (*Stepping up*) What do you want to ask?

REPORTER. Ah, Mr. Mayor, your honor. As you know, people are protesting on your curb about some of your unusual behavior this morning. It seems that you laughed out loud during the funeral of Mr. Victor Jordan.

CHARLES. That wasn't exactly laughter . . .

REPORTER. Reports from several sources say that it was indeed a very disrespectful laughter which interestingly enough came on the same day that it was discovered that Mr. Jordan had recently lost an extremely large amount of money.

CHARLES. (*Sincerely confused*) What?

REPORTER. And that he had over the past three months been calling one number more than any other, a number assigned to his home.

CHARLES. What?

DANA. The mayor will answer questions for you at a later time.

REPORTER. Mr. Mayor, do you have anything to say?

DANA. No comment, Charles.

CHARLES. Exactly. No comment. I will talk with you later, after I've researched the facts.

REPORTER. Are you claiming to be unaware of any of this new information?

CHARLES. You're darn right, that's what I'm claiming.

REPORTER. And you didn't laugh at this man's funeral?

CHARLES. I got a frog in my throat.

REPORTER. Is that your official stance?

CHARLES. That. And that I'm still holding the goose.

REPORTER. Pardon?

CHARLES. No comment.

REPORTER. Why is there a shirtless young man lying on your living room floor?

CHARLES. Swimming lessons.

REPORTER. What? Oh! Alex Lee Moore? Lauren Manchester? What are . . .?

ALEX LEE. Want to see me shirtless?

LAUREN. They have before. A lot.

REPORTER. I just want to ask . . .

CHARLES. Good day. (*He closes the door on the reporter.*)

DANA. Oh, my.

CHARLES. What's going on?

DANA. I told you they knew it was laughter.

ALEX LEE. What an interesting home this is.

MARGOT. I was about to say the same thing.

There is a knock on the door. Durry enters.

DURRY. What's going on?

DANA. Finally. You're back. Please do your job and answer the door.

DURRY. Come. Go. Leave. Stay. I don't know what you people want of me.

DANA. Just a little respect.

DURRY. Listen.

APRIL. Oh, I'm sure that's not all people want of you.

The knock is louder.

DANA. Durry, would you get the door?

Detective Olan Chamberlain and Police Officers AJ Hankins and Terry Blaylock are at the door.

DURRY. May I help you?

CHAM. Yes, I'm Detective Olan Chamberlain, and these are Officers Hankins and Blaylock. I need to speak with the mayor if at all possible.

DURRY. I'll see if he's in.

CHARLES. Of course, I'm in. They can see me standing right here. Come in, Detective. Is there something I can help you with?

CHAM. (*Looking around*) It seems that I have come at a busy time.

CHARLES. That's every minute of every day, Detective. You know: doing the people's work.

CHAM. Yes. The people's work. There are quite a few of us paid to do that. May I ask who these people are?

CHARLES. Well, this is my once-lovely wife, Dana. My daughter, April. Her pseudo-boyfriend, Rex. Their friend, William. This is my assistant in domestic issues, Durry Durrant. You may know Mayor Margot Schmitt, from our German sister city, Düsseldorf, and her son, Wilhelm. Uh, long story. And you must know Alex Lee Moore and Lauren Manchester, the actors. They are here to discuss the upcoming performing arts center.

CHAM. Ah, the performing arts center you're betting your campaign on.

CHARLES. Well, that's partially true, now that you put it that way, Detective Chamberlain. Wait a minute. You're not related to Tim Chamberlain, are you?

CHAM. As a matter of fact, he's my brother, Mr. Bagley.

DANA. The Tim Chamberlain running against Charles for mayor?

CHAM. The same.

DANA. Well, I must protest. Any reason that you may have for being here surely is dwarfed by the fact that you have a familial bias against my husband.

CHAM. First, are you under the assumption that your husband has participated in any kind of criminal activity that make me question his honesty and allow me to exhibit any bias.

DANA. Of course not.

CHAM. Well, you don't have anything to worry about then. Second, I have a job to do, and as a detective with this city, over which by the way your husband presides, I am bound by duty to pursue any and everything that I feel may be criminal. If your husband is or is not guilty of something, it is not my job to make that decision. I am here to investigate. That is not for or against Mr. Bagley. Does that make sense?

DANA. I suppose.

CHAM. Good. Third, I hate my brother and hope he rots in hell. He stole my second wife, the only pretty woman I ever married, and I have never nor will ever forgive him for that. On that level, not only do I not want him to win the mayoral election (which will then force me to leave this fair city) but I will also be voting for your husband as I simultaneously wish the eternal flames of hell on Tim. How's that?

DANA. Fair enough?

CHAM. Fair enough.

CHARLES. How may I help you?

CHAM.   Well, we have a few problems we need to figure out, a few puzzles I need to solve.

CHARLES.   Of course. Anything I can do to help.

CHAM.   Today, you attended the funeral of Mr. Victor Jordan.

CHARLES.   Yes, my wife and I did attend.

CHAM.   And at that funeral, did you find anything humorous.

DANA.   Good Lord.

CHAM.   Pardon?

DANA.   Told you so. Told you so. Told you so. Told you so.

CHAM.   What is she talking about, Mr. Bagley?

CHARLES.   (*Deep breath*) Well, I know it was disrespectful and I know I've denied it to the press, but yes, I did laugh.

CHAM.   May I ask why?

CHARLES.   Is it a crime to laugh in public?

CHAM.   Not at all. It's just pieces in a bigger puzzle. I am not hear to condemn a man for laughing.

CHARLES.   (*to Dana*) See?

CHAM.   But I am curious as to why you laughed.

CHARLES.   A few minutes prior to the viewing of the body, the widow, Mrs. Jordan, slipped and busted her derrière on the floor. I held the laughter in for as long as I could, but when I got to Victor with the little smile on his face, I lost it.

APRIL.   Daddy!

MARGOT.   Charles, you didn't?

CHARLES.   Yes, I did. It was funny. Okay?

REX.   Sounds reasonable to me.

CHARLES.   Shut up.

CHAM.   And Mr. Bagley. Are you aware of some other things we have found out about Mr. Jordan today?

CHARLES.   Well, a noisy reporter from the Post came by and mentioned something about Jordan losing money recently.

CHAM.   Yes, and about some phone calls made to and from this residence.

CHARLES.   That's what the reporter said, but I swear to you that I was as shocked to hear that as was anyone. I have no idea how that could even be true.

DANA.   Nor do I. I promise Charles that I have never had any contact with Mr. Jordan outside of your relationship with him, dinner parties, city functions.

CHAM.   You must admit: the money, the calls, and today's laughter all make for some oddly connected clues.

CHARLES.   I can see how that looks, but I can assure you that we know nothing about it and will cooperate with you fully.

CHAM.   That's good to hear. (*Pause*) You know we have also had some interesting events downtown earlier this morning as well which coincidently involve Mr. Moore and Ms. Manchester who, again coincidently, just happen to be here.

CHARLES.   You mean the movie poster shootings.

CHAM.   Yes, someone or several "someones" have been reeking some havoc by shooting stars right there in the posters at local cinemas. The last few faces have been of Mr. Moore and Ms. Manchester.

ALEX LEE.   We were discussing that very issue with Mr. Bagley earlier. It makes us uneasy and puts in jeopardy our association with the performing arts center we had been eagerly backing.

CHAM.   Is that how you feel as well, Ms. Manchester?

LAUREN.   Yes.

CHAM.   I see.

CHARLES.   Well, do you have any leads?

CHAM.   As a matter of fact, that's another reason I'm here.

DANA.   Leads? Here?

CHAM. Ironically, yes. We seem to think the perpetrators, well it all has to do with a German. . .

MARGOT. German?

CHAM. Yes, a German . . .

WILHELM. Wait a minute. What are you saying?

MARGOT. Why is it when something violent happens, people automatically blame it on the Germans?

CHAM. Mrs. Schmitt, if you'll allow me to finish. I didn't say a German person. I was trying to say a little German-made car . . .

MARGOT. Oh.

WILHELM. I'll just sit now.

CHAM. A little yellow German Mercedes.

CHARLES. A yellow Mercedes.

DANA. Like . . .

APRIL. You mean . . .

ALEX LEE. (*looking out*) Like . . .

CHAM. Yes, (*looking at Rex*) like the one sitting in the driveway. Do I have to ask to whom this fine car belongs?

REX. There's no need. You know it's mine.

CHAM. Indeed, I do. It seems a yellow Mercedes exactly matching this car was seen at 2 a.m. this morning in front of the Cinema Ten on Harrison. Gun fire was heard. The car spun away. And the faces of Mr. Moore and Ms. Manchester were shot out with a 9mm Glock 17.

ALEX LEE. Oh really.

HANKINS. Yes, really.

CHAM. Hankins.

HANKINS. Sorry, Detective.

CHAM.   You know, there aren't that many bright yellow Mercedes around here.

REX.   I'm sure there were several on the assembly line.

CHAM.   Surely. But not many on the streets. For many reasons.

DANA.   I often wondered how you could afford a Mercedes.

CHAM.   Wonderment is the key to breaking crime, Mrs. Bagley. The wonderment of a child.

APRIL.   May I go to the restroom?

CHAM.   This isn't a school, Ms. Bagley. Of course, you may. We don't have hall passes and
        hall monitors. Hankins, escort her to the lavatory, would you?

HANKINS. Yes, sir. (*They leave.*)

CHAM.   Back to the mystery at hand. A yellow Mercedes. A college student. A shooting of the
        faces of movie stars on the side of a cinema. A dead entrepreneur. A mystery indeed.
        Seemingly nothing connects, but it all must. It has to.

REX.   Or you may be fabricating meaning out of desired theory?

CHAM.   Ah, an educated man. I like that. A lover of philosophy. Hmmm. Interesting.
        Philosophy that is. I remember studying a little philosophy when I was at Harvard.
        Interesting how words can be twisted and ideas manipulated as the philosopher sees fit.
        Sort of like Plato's Allegory of the Cave, all those shadows cast on the cave wall,
        images of the echoes of reality, but never the real thing. Accept in this case, these
        simple black and white shadows are shattered by a yellow Mercedes and an eye
        witness.

REX.   I'm not your adversary. I just am not guilty of what you are assuming.

CHAM.   Assumption's a dangerous thing, Mr. Walters. Is it REX Walters, isn't it?

REX.   Yes, sir, it is.

CHAM.   Well, Mr. Walters, I'm not your adversary either. I am a detective investigating a crime,
        well, a series of crimes I guess now. And the only adversary I have is what comes
        against truth--and of course, the actual perpetrator.

REX.   Of course.

CHAM.   Mr. Durrant.

DURRY. Yes, sir.

CHAM. Do you have any coffee made?

DURRY. Yes, sir. Would you like some?

CHAM. So polite. No, thank you, but I would like for the rest of you to go to the kitchen area and enjoy a nice cup of coffee while I talk with Mr. Walters a few minutes. Officer Blaylock, would you join these fine people in the kitchen.

BLAYLOCK. Certainly, sir. If you'd come with me.

They exit.

CHAM. So, Mr. Walters.

REX. Yes, sir.

CHAM. Could you tell me where you were last night about 2 a.m.?

REX. I was at my apartment.

CHAM. Do you have any witnesses to that effect?

REX. My friend, William, who you just sent out. He was with me. If you'll allow me, I can go get him to . . .

CHAM. No, that'll be alright. I can speak with Mr. Baines in a few minutes if need be.

REX. So, you know all of our names?

CHAM. What kind of detective would I be if I didn't do my homework? What would be a reason for someone to shoot out the faces of movie stars, do you think?

REX. I wouldn't know.

CHAM. Could you speculate?

REX. You mean assume?

CHAM. Yes, I see your point. But why would someone do that? For fun?

REX. Possibly.

CHAM. Or to make some sort of point?

REX. Possibly.

CHAM. But with a Glock. That's quite a point.

REX. You know it's a Glock?

CHAM. Oh, yes. Our investigative researchers are quite the impressive lot. We have a lot of things narrowed down.

REX. I didn't know we were so CSI around here.

CHAM. Oh, we're many things around here. Did you know Victor Jordan?

REX. Pardon me?

CHAM. I'm sorry. Did I stutter? Victor Jordan? Did you know him?

REX. No, sir. I'm just a college student. I don't get the opportunity to hob nob with the likes of Victor Jordan.

APRIL appears in the doorway, eavesdropping.

CHAM. But you are here at the home of the mayor. You must get the opportunity to meet some pretty amazing people

REX. Not yet.

CHAM. Yet?

REX. I mean . . .

CHAM. You mean "not yet." You have aspirations, dreams. (*Rex is silent.*) Of course, you do. You're an intelligent young man, hoping to be influential, important. And it doesn't hurt to be in love with the daughter of the mayor himself.

REX. I never said I was in love with her.

CHAM. Oh, okay. So, you're not?

REX. I just . . .

CHAM. You're just here for something. And you have a lot of circumstantial evidence piling up against you. There's something going on. It's amazing what people will do for love.

REX. I said I don't love her.

CHAM. The passion that people feel causes them to do crazy things.

REX. I don't love her! She's convenient.

CHAM. Oh, I see.

REX. It's hard to explain.

CHAM. No need to try. You just did.

REX. Listen.

CHAM. Mr. Baines can attest to your whereabouts this morning you say?

REX. Yes. I'm sure he'll remember.

CHAM. I'm sure he will. Blaylock! You can bring everyone back in!

April stumbles in. Rex is unaware that she has heard any of his statements. Hankins follows April.

HANKINS. Sir, I dozed at the bathroom door a bit. I apologize.

CHAM. No need for apologies, Hankins. You might have a touch of narcolepsy. It worked out.

Everyone else enters.

REX. April, you okay?

She ignores him. William enters and stands semi-close to April. He seems to be able to tell that something is wrong with her.

CHARLES. Is everything alright, Detective? Is there anything that I need to know?

CHAM. I think I am starting to put two and two together.

DANA. Thank Heaven.

DURRY. Yeah. Thank Heaven.

CHARLES. So, is the answer four?

CHAM. I think right now it's 3.8. It's about to be four, though.

ALEX LEE. I want to know if this man has been the one shooting out my face every night. I have a right to know if my life is in jeopardy. Oh yeah, and hers, too.

CHAM. Well . . .

MARGOT. And I need to know if there is something going on that could cause detriment to our cities' friendship.

WILHELM. Ya! We want the Olympics. Every sport. Even diving.

CHARLES. Please stop.

CHAM. I think it will all make sense once . . .

The door opens and in storms Bethany, dressed very oddly, like a villainess of some sort.

BETHANY. Ah, just in time I see.

DANA. Bethany, this definitely is not the time. Leave.

CHARLES. Bethany, go home.

BETHANY. I'm not Bethany. I tell you this all the time. I am Valencia Love, keeper of evil and avenger of the weak, downtrodden, and unknown.

CHAM. What's this?

CHARLES. Next-door neighbor. Mental issues.

BETHANY. Speak not lies! I avenge those who cannot avenge themselves. I see things. I know things. I look in shrubs and under bricks and find what I need to carry out what's right.

CHAM. What is she talking about?

WILLIAM. Shrubs?

BETHANY. And you are the rich and famous Alex Lee Moore.

ALEX LEE. Well, she's not stupid.

BETHANY. And for that you must die.

Bethany pulls out the Glock that William hid by the driveway and points it at Alex Lee.

BETHANY. Die, movie star.

She fires. Alex Lee tries to leap out of the way. There is a frenzy of movement as the whole room goes in disarray and Bethany is subdued by the officers.

BETHANY. Let me go.

CHAM. Not until we figure out what's happening

In the struggle, the gun has fallen to the floor. April has picked it up. She looks at it.

REX. Good job, sweetheart. Now, give me the gun.

APRIL. No. (*She points it at Rex.*)

CHAM. April, put down the gun.

Hankins and Blaylock draw their firearms.

APRIL. No.

Alex Lee stands up. Holding his shoulder.

ALEX LEE. I'm alive, but I have flesh wound on my shoulder.

Everyone ignores him, looking at April.

DANA. Don't point your guns at her!

CHAM. Down with the guns, officers. April, I need you to give me that gun.

APRIL. Not yet. Rex?

REX. What, baby?

APRIL. Don't call me "baby."

REX. But . . .

APRIL. I said, "Don't call me 'baby.'"

REX. Okay. What's wrong? Why are you pointing that gun at me?

APRIL. Don't love me, huh?

REX. What?

APRIL. I'm convenient?

REX. Oh, April. I was just . . .

APRIL. I heard you.

REX. I was just . . .

APRIL. No more lies. Did you ever love me?

REX. April.

APRIL. It's a simple question, and I want a simple answer. I know you don't love me now, but did you ever love me?

REX. April.

April points the gun at his crotch.

APRIL. (*Raising her voice*) Did you?!

REX. No. Not . . . love. No.

APRIL. So, you lied all this time?

REX. April.

APRIL. (*Raising her voice again*) You lied?!

REX. Sorta.

APRIL. Sorta?!

REX. Yes, I did.

APRIL. Why? But no, I don't have to ask. I think I already know. You wanted the kind of life that being close to the Bagleys could give you.

REX. I . . .

APRIL. Even if it meant doing anything to get it. (*Pause.*) So, let's really see if I am thinking up to your par now, Mr. Philosopher.

REX. April . . .

APRIL. Over the course of several months, I have walked into this living room and even my old bedroom to find you on the phone talking very seriously. And I bet I know who was on the other end of that line now.

REX. There is no need of you . . .

APRIL. Mr. Victor Jordan. The reason all those calls were from here and all that money missing from Jordan was because you were blackmailing him.

REX. April, that's enough.

APRIL. (*She puts the gun to his head.*) AM I RIGHT?!

REX. (*Fearful*) YES!

APRIL. There. There is it. You interned for Harper and Grant, you saw his briefings, and you knew that he was trying to stop Daddy from building his Center?

CHARLES. What?

CHAM. Excellent.

APRIL. So, he paid you to keep your mouth shut and to help him out by scaring people with the poster shootings. No one would want to help with the Center--with the stigma of the shootings.

REX. You've made a major mistake.

APRIL. I've made several. But this isn't one of them.

CHAM. April, drop the gun. We have our man now. We know.

April points it at his chest. Then she drops it.

Blaylock picks it up.

CHAM. Well, well. It's quite an interesting web we have here.

REX. It's going to get a lot more tangled. I hate to burst your bubble for the future, April, but I wasn't in this alone. I'll have you know . . .

Gunshot. Rex falls to the floor. Everyone looks around. Durry is standing, holding a gun.

DURRY. I told you. I take care of things.

DANA. DURRY!

CHARLES. Durry?!

He drops the gun. The officers subdue him. Chamberlain checks on Rex.

CHAM. He's dead.

DANA. You know, I wished it, but I didn't mean it.

CHARLES. I did.

DANA. Durry, why?

DURRY. It was the right thing to do.

CHAM. Mr. Durrant, who are you protecting? What was he going to say?

LAUREN. He was going to lie. He was like all villains, never taking responsibility for their own evil actions, always trying to bring someone else down so as not to look so bad, trying to save his own butt. He was about to murder an innocent person with the power of his tongue, a crime people in my profession fall victim to every day. He was about to kill.

CHAM. Well-put, Ms. Manchester. Well-put. But the fact remains that Mr. Durrant just committed an act of cold-blooded murder and will have to suffer the consequences.

DURRY. I'm aware of that.

DANA. Oh, Durry.

APRIL. Are you sad, Mother?

DANA. What do you mean?

APRIL. You know exactly what I mean.

MARGOT. (*Understanding*) You mean, April, that your mother is worried about Durry going to prison because he saved you from the like of Rex here, and that you know that secretly Durry, your mother, and I have been working on a major project to raise money for your father's Center, and that we were going to surprise him, but now we can't?

APRIL. A secret project?

CHARLES. A secret project?

MARGOT. That you heard us discussing?

APRIL. That I heard you . . . ? Oh. (*embarrassed*) Oh, Mom. A secret project?

DANA. Yes, dear.

April hugs her.

ALEX LEE. I'm still bleeding here.

BETHANY. I am Valencia!

WILHELM. Shut up.

CHAM. I think it's time we get all this cleaned up.

HANKINS. Yes, sir.

CHAM. We need to get the morgue out here to pick up Mr. Walters. We need to take Mr. Durrant out to the car, and yes, Ms. Bethany needs to come down to the station as well.

BETHANY. (*Excited*) Delighted!!!

CHAM. And we'll need to call your mother.

BETHANY. Oh.

CHAM. Blaylock, we also need to call an ambulance for Mr. Moore.

ALEX LEE. Someone knows I'm alive.

CHARLES. Knowing and caring are two separate things.

Lauren laughs.

ALEX LEE. What are you laughing at?

LAUREN. I'm hungry.

ALEX LEE. That doesn't make sense.

LAUREN. I don't care. You don't make sense.

The officers take Durry and Bethany out.

DANA. Good-bye, Durry. We'll come see you.

CHARLES. Yeah. Good-bye, Champ. I'll call my lawyers in a few minutes.

DURRY. God help me.

BETHANY. I wish to thank the members of the Academy. You love me. You really, really love me!

CHAM. Quite an afternoon. Quite an . . . well, it's really evening now.

CHARLES. Yes.

CHAM. You know: in a few minutes, this is going to turn into a media circus. Things are not going to be pretty.

CHARLES. You're right. It's about to be rough. It won't look good on my campaign.

CHAM. True.

CHARLES. Your brother may win.

CHAM. (*Crestfallen*) I'll do my best to keep the publicity down to a minimum. I like it here.

CHARLES. Thank you.

CHAM. We'll be out here if you need us.

CHARLES. (*Shaking his hand*) Thank you.

Chamberlain leaves.

Charles, Dana, Margot, Alex Lee, Lauren, and Wilhelm sit. William and April remain standing. All avoid the corpse, now covered with a sheet.

WILLIAM. (*to April*) You okay?

APRIL. Yeah. I think so.

DANA. I'm in shock.

MARGOT. I'm at a loss for words.

LAUREN. I'm still hungry.

ALEX LEE. You never eat.

LAUREN. Exactly. I'm hungry.

DANA. Well, we have plenty to eat in the kitchen.

APRIL. Care to walk with me a bit?

WILLIAM. Sure.

APRIL. We're going to step out on the terrace.

CHARLES. Don't go far. We need to be where Detective Chamberlain can talk to us. They still
have a lot to wrap up tonight.

APRIL. We'll be just out on the terrace.

*April and William exit to the terrace, which is downstage right. The living room and the terrace
scenes occur simultaneously.*

CHARLES. I like that kid.

ALEX LEE. She's your daughter. You're supposed to like her.

CHARLES. I'm talking about William.

DANA. You know that when Rex was about . . .

CHARLES. Stop. Remember: fathers have those lies they have to tell themselves. Let it be.

DANA. I understand.

WILLIAM. Are you sure you're okay?

APRIL. I don't think I've been more okay in a long time.

DANA. There's a dead man in my living room.

MARGOT. Oh, I had almost forgotten that.

DANA. Strangely, I'm not really sad.

APRIL. Strangely, I'm not really sad.

ALEX LEE. This is surrealism at its ultimate.

WILHELM. What does that mean?

CHARLES. Things are weird, but okay.

WILLIAM. Things are weird, but they're going to be okay.

MARGOT. What do we do now?

APRIL. What do we do now?

CHARLES. I think we have to wait on the police to talk with us. As long as we don't leave, I think we're okay.

WILLIAM. I think we're okay. Look, April, I have something I need to tell you.

CHARLES. I think our best bet is to go get a bite to eat.

APRIL. Look! William! A shooting star!

WILLIAM. It sure was. Wow.

APRIL. Is that an omen or a sign?

WILLIAM. It's what it needs to be for us. We make choices, APRIL. And I need to tell you . . .

APRIL. Stop. Do you love me?

WILLIAM. I . . .

APRIL. Don't think. Do you love me?

WILLIAM. Yes.

APRIL. Really, really love me?

WILLIAM. For a long time, yes.

APRIL. I believe you.

Wilhelm stands.

WILHELM. Or what we CAN do is go out to the pool for an evening swim! (*He starts to remove his clothing.*)

All at once, the others stand and move toward the kitchen--saying "I'm hungry," "Food sounds food," etc.

WILHELM. (*Still removing clothes as they leave*) No wait! We can swim. You know how we swim in Germany! You know I have a nice body!

WILLIAM. We'll face this one day at a time.

APRIL. But now it'll make a lot more sense. Now kiss me.

WILLIAM. Are you narrating?

APRIL. Absolutely.

They kiss.

WILHELM. (*Now at his boxers*) Where did everyone go? Oh, what a pretty star! (*He passes out from narcolepsy and starts snoring.*)

Lowery Christopher Collins (Chris) has been an educator and writer for over thirty years. He is currently a professor of English at Panola College in Carthage, Texas. He has taught at the high school, middle school, and elementary school levels and as an English and literature instructor at the college and university level. For several years, he was a high school theatre director and a gifted education consultant. He's been honored with several teaching awards, including the Young Audiences of Northeast Texas Outstanding Service to the Profession Award and the Kennedy Center's Steven Sondheim Award for being one of the most "Inspirational Teachers" in the U.S.

He is also an award-winning playwright of over thirty scripts, a weekly newspaper columnist, a short story writer, a poet, a pianist, a vocalist, a songwriter, a recording artist with Daywind Studios, the founder and artistic director of Stagelands Theatre Company, an aspiring novelist, and a (former) choir director. He's taught a variety of classes, from rhetoric and composition to literature to acting to the Bible.

He holds a Bachelor of Arts Degree in English and History and a Master of Arts Degree in English from Stephen F. Austin State University in Texas and has served on fine arts and gifted education committees as well as on a board of governors for a small playhouse.

In addition to his interests in teaching, directing, and writing, he has a fondness for lighthouses, windmills, filmmaking, salsa, sculpture, Flannery O'Connor, travel, dominos, guacamole, social media, genetics, Maine, landscaping, pillows, gospel music, Shakespeare, marbles, YouTube, quantum physics, movies, weird jokes, maps, trees, cold rooms, and Texas.

He can be reached at mrchriscollins@hotmail.com,

on Facebook at www.facebook.com/tofferdreams,

on Twitter at "tofferdreams,"

and at his website: www.ChristopherCollinsOnline.com.

To view Christopher Collins's books and other writing, visit Ponderlake Publishing, at www.ponderlake.com.

www.ingramcontent.com/pod-product-compliance
Lightning Source LLC
Chambersburg PA
CBHW020600130626
46552CB00007B/2967